Rumpelstiltskin

retold by Diane Stortz

Fairy Tale Classics

LANDOLL
Ashland, Ohio 44805
© The Landoll Apple logo is a trademark owned by Landoll, Inc.
and is registered in the U.S. Patent and Trademark Office.

ong ago, there lived a tailor who was known for his bragging...even about things that were not true. This man's talk got his beautiful young daughter into a great deal of trouble. The story would not have a happy ending at all, if not for a faithful servant and a funny little man named... but that's what this story is about.

One day, the tailor happened to see the king riding through town. The man wanted to make himself seem important, so he called to the king, "I have a daughter who can spin straw into gold!" The king stopped at once. "That is an art that pleases me!" he said. The king was a greedy man who was never happy and always wanted more. "Bring your daughter to the castle tomorrow," the king told the tailor. "And I will put her to a test."

he next day, the tailor took his beautiful daughter to the castle. Of course she did not know how to spin straw into gold, but she was shown into a room filled with straw. The king gave her a spinning wheel and a spindle. "Now, to work!" he said. "If all this straw isn't gold by morning, you will never see your father again." Then the king left and locked the door.

The poor girl sat down on the straw and began to cry. Then the door opened again, and a funny little man came into the room.

ood evening, dear girl," said the little man. "Why are you crying?"

"I am supposed to spin straw into gold for the king," said the girl. "And I don't know how." "Oh, but I know how," said the little man. "What will you give me if I spin it for you?" "My necklace," said the girl.

The little man took the necklace and sat down at the spinning wheel. In seconds, the first spool was full of golden thread. The tailor's daughter fell asleep. When the straw was turned to gold, the little man disappeared.

n the morning at sunrise, the king returned. When he saw the golden spools, he was pleased. But because he was greedy, he took the girl to a larger room filled with more straw. "Spin all this straw into gold by morning if you want to see your father again," said the king. Then he left and locked the door.

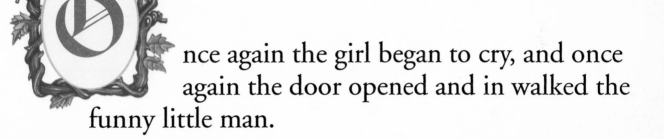

nce again the girl began to cry, and once again the door opened and in walked the funny little man.

"What will you give me if I spin the straw into gold for you this time?" he asked.
"The gold ring on my finger," said the girl.
The little man took the ring and began to work.
By morning all the straw was spun into gold.

The king came at sunrise. "Wonderful, my dear!" he cried. But the greedy king wanted still more. He locked the girl in an even bigger room full of straw and told her, "Spin all this straw into gold tonight. If you do, you shall become my wife."

When the king was gone, the little man came again. "What will you give me this time if I spin the straw into gold for you?"

"I have nothing left to give you," the girl said sadly. "Then promise to give me your first child after you become queen," said the little man. The tailor's daughter did not believe the king would really marry her. So she promised the little man her first child. In the morning, the king found the room full of gold, and he married the tailor's daughter.

he next year, the queen gave birth to a beautiful child. She was happy, and had forgotten the funny little man. But suddenly he appeared and said, "Now give me what you promised."

The queen was horrified. She offered the little man all the treasure of the kingdom instead. "No," said the little man. "Something living is more important than all the treasure in the world."

Then the queen began to grieve and weep and could not be consoled. The little man began to feel sorry for her. "I will give you three days," he said. "If you can guess my name by the third day, you may keep your child."

he queen spent the night making a list of every name she had ever known. Then she sent a servant out into the kingdom to make a list of names she had never heard before.

When the little man appeared again that evening, the queen began to call out the names one at a time. "Are you Tom? Dick? Harry?" she asked. But after every name the little man shook his head.

"Are you Gaspar? Melchior? Balthasar?" The little man just smiled and said, "That's not my name." The next day the queen sent her servant out into the kingdom to search for unusual names, like Ribsofbeef or Muttonchops or Lacedleg.

But when the little man appeared that evening, he just shook his head and said again and again, "That's not my name."

n the third day, the queen was in despair. She sent her servant out into the kingdom one last time. When he came back, the servant said, "I climbed a high mountain, where the fox and the hare say good night to each other at the edge of the forest. There I saw a small cottage, and in front of the cottage was a fire. And in front of the fire danced a funny little man. He hopped about on one leg, singing,

"Today I'll brew, tomorrow I'll bake.
Soon I'll have the queen's namesake.
Oh, how hard it is to play my game,
For Rumpelstiltskin is my name!"

hen the queen heard this, she began to dance herself, for joy. When the little man appeared that evening she asked him, "Is your name Kunz?" "No!" said the little man. "Is your name Heinz?" "No!" said the little man. He began to reach for the queen's sleeping child. "Is your name Rumpelstiltskin?" asked the queen.

"Who told you? Who told you?" howled the little man. He jumped around screeching and stomping his feet so hard that he stomped right through the floor and disappeared. And that was the last time anyone ever saw Rumpelstiltskin.